A Flower for Gran

Practising long vowel phonemes,
CVCC and CCVC plus polysyllabic words

First published in 2007 by
Franklin Watts
338 Euston Road
London
NW1 3BH

Franklin Watts Australia
Level 17/207 Kent Street
Sydney
NSW 2000

A CIP catalogue record for this book is available
from the British Library.

ISBN: 978 0 7496 7130 3 (hbk)
ISBN: 978 0 7496 7317 8 (pbk)

Series Editor: Jackie Hamley
Series Advisors: Dr Barrie Wade, Dr Hilary Minns
Series Designer: Peter Scoulding

Printed in China

Franklin Watts is a division of
Hachette Children's Books.

A Flower
for Gran

by
Margaret Nash

Illustrated by
Stefania Colnaghi

W

FRANKLIN WATTS
LONDON•SYDNEY

Margaret Nash
"I once planted a seed which turned out to be the same flower as the one in this story. The birds were very pleased with it. They ate all the seeds from the centre of the flower!"

Stefania Colnaghi
"I live near Pavia in Italy. I love walking in the hills with my dogs and seeing the wild flowers."

Dad was outside in the garden.

"Come and see this!"
said Dad.

8

There was a new green shoot pushing out of the soil! It was very small.

We ran upstairs to tell
Gran about the shoot.

11

Gran had no garden.

She only had a window box.

Gran had a look out of the window to see the shoot.

"You must speak to it," said Gran. "Then it might grow to be a big flower."

She made Dad laugh.
"All right," he said.
"We will!"

We both told the shoot
to grow, and I fed it.

The sun and rain fed it, too.

Soon there was a leaf.

"Grow as tall as the wall," I said. "As high as the sky," Dad said.

22

"Grow high, but pop in
to see me!" said Gran.

The shoot went up ...

... and up ...

24

... and UP!

Then the next time Gran went
to open her window, it was there.
It almost went inside!

"Well! Hello, you big, yellow sunflower!" said Gran.

"I shall enjoy you!"

And she did!

Notes for parents and teachers

READING CORNER PHONICS has been structured to provide maximum support for children learning to read through synthetic phonics. The stories are designed for independent reading but may also be used by adults for sharing with young children.

The teaching of early reading through synthetic phonics focuses on the 44 sounds in the English language, and how these sounds correspond to their written form in the 26 letters of the alphabet. Carefully controlled vocabulary makes these books accessible for children at different stages of phonics teaching, progressing from simple CVC (consonant-vowel-consonant) words such as "top" (t-o-p) to trisyllabic words such as "messenger" (mess-en-ger). READING CORNER PHONICS allows children to read words in context, and also provides visual clues and repetition to further support their reading. These books will help develop the all important confidence in the new reader, and encourage a love of reading that will last a lifetime!

If you are reading this book with a child, here are a few tips:

1. Talk about the story before you start reading. Look at the cover and the title. What might the story be about? Why might the child like it?

2. Encourage the child to reread the story, and to retell the story in their own words, using the illustrations to remind them what has happened.

3. Discuss the story and see if the child can relate it to their own experience, or perhaps compare it to another story they know.

4. Give praise! Small mistakes need not always be corrected. If a child is stuck on a word, ask them to try and sound it out and then blend it together again, or model this yourself. For example "wish" w-i-sh "wish".

READING CORNER PHONICS covers two grades of synthetic phonics teaching, with three levels at each grade. Each level has a certain number of words per story, indicated by the number of bars on the spine of the book:

GRADE 1

50 words — CVC words with short vowel sounds

70 words — CVC words plus sounds of more than one letter

100 words — Sounds of more than one letter, simple polysyllabic words

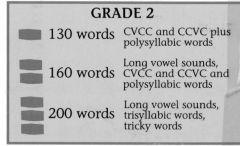

GRADE 2

130 words — CVCC and CCVC plus polysyllabic words

160 words — Long vowel sounds, CVCC and CCVC and polysyllabic words

200 words — Long vowel sounds, trisyllabic words, tricky words